SHADOW
and the
Halloween Party
by Andy Rector

Illustrated by
Gerry Oliviera

Shadow was a kitten. He liked to run and romp and play. But Shadow had no one to play with most of the time. Shadow was lonely.

One day Shadow saw something move in the grass.

He snuck over to find out what it was. "Who are you?" Shadow asked the tiny creature. The tiny creature jumped with surprise. "Go away," it said.

"I want to be friends," said Shadow.

"Kittens and mice are not friends," said the tiny creature.

"Are you a 'mice'?" asked Shadow.

"No," said the tiny creature. "I am a mouse. My name is Squeek. I'm dressed up as a cowboy. I'm going to a Halloween Party."

"May I go?" asked Shadow.
"If you go," said Squeek,
"you must be my horse. All cow-
boys have horses." And Squeek
climbed onto Shadow's back.

Squeek and Shadow rode up to the house. "Follow me," said Squeek. "The party is through here."

Shadow followed Squeek. Shadow barely fit through the hole, but he made it. Shadow found a party going on inside. Mice were dressed up in costumes.

Suddenly someone yelled,
"A kitten! A kitten! Run!"
All the mice ran and hid. But
Squeek did not run and hide.

"Don't worry, everyone," said Squeek. "I heard that kittens and mice are not friends. But it's not true. This is Shadow. He is my friend."

Slowly the mice came out from hiding. When they found out how nice Shadow was, everyone wanted to be his friend.

The mice even let Shadow judge a costume contest. It was the best time Shadow ever had. Shadow and Squeek became best friends.